Babba and I Went Hunting Today

...and God sent a sunset 'cause my Babba is sick

Stacy Barton

Illustrated by Maureen O'Brien

KREGEL Kidzone

Where Kids are number One

Babba and I Went Hunting Today

Text © 2004 by Stacy Barton
Illustrations © 2004 by Maureen O'Brien

Published by Kregel Kidzone, an imprint of Kregel Publications, P.O. Box 2607, Grand Rapids, MI 49501.

Art Direction / Interior Design: John M. Lucas

ISBN 0-8254-2037-7

Printed in China

For all the Babbas in my life
who have fought the darkness
and seen God paint the sky
and for all the Honeys
who have held my hand in the park.

For my love, Todd, and my babies,
Whitney, Meredith, Taylor, and Olivia.

My Babba is funny, she dances and sings.
She loves noisy jewelry and wears lots of rings.

Her eyes smile green,
they are always the same.
But she lost all her hair
when her sickness came.

Some days are good days
and some days are bad.

Some days Babba's tired
or silly or sad.

This morning (it's Tuesday),
"Let's go hunting!" she said.
So we put on blue beads and
tied scarves on our heads.

"For what?" I replied, as we
skipped through the door.
"Don't know yet, Honey.
We have to explore!"

Adventures with Babba are always exciting,
because she can find things without even trying.
We jumped over cracks in the sidewalk path.

And hunted **big** tigers.

And laughed . . .

and laughed.

We sneaked through the park
and peeked in the fountain.

Then climbed up the hill
like it was a mountain.
Babba said, "Look!" and made
a scope with her hands,
and we looked down like pirates
who'd conquered new lands.

Then we laid on our backs
in the prickly grass,
and saw pictures there in
the clouds floating past.

I scooted real close, because
Babba smells good,
like soft-soap and lavender,
as all Babbas should.

We stayed there all day, just hunting around.
I found pebbles and pine cones by trees
on the ground.

We sat on the hill as the sun went down,
and called out the colors just for the sound!

Then Babba said, "Honey, go find me a stick."
And I ran for the trees and brought one back quick.

She slipped off her scarf and made it a flag
that we pushed in the earth so the stick wouldn't sag.

We watched as the sky turned from pink into purple,
and Babba's scarf flew on the stick in a circle.

Then Babba said softly,
"We found it," and smiled
as I rubbed her smooth head
and leaned close for awhile.

"What is it?" I asked her. "What did we find?"
"God," whispered Babba. "He painted a sign."

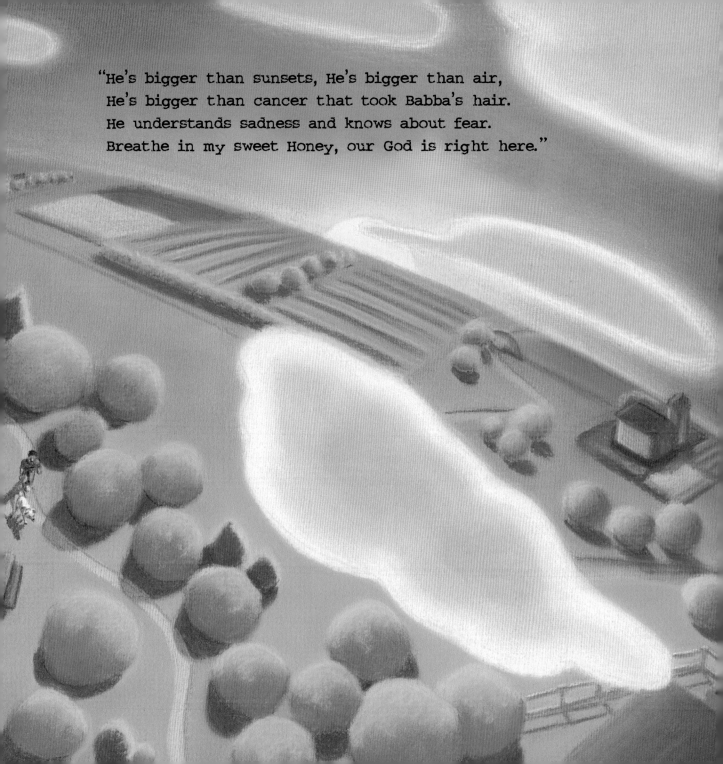

"He's bigger than sunsets, He's bigger than air,
He's bigger than cancer that took Babba's hair.
He understands sadness and knows about fear.
Breathe in my sweet Honey, our God is right here."

"Are you sad?" I asked Babba,
because I saw tears.
"Sometimes," she answered,
"but I'm losing my fears."

I crawled in her lap and
we watched our God paint,
and we counted the stars
until it got late.

Then we climbed down the hill
to go home in the dark,
and skipped down the sidewalk,
right through the park.

From the porch of her house
we saw on the hill
Babba's scarf on the stick,
dancing there still.

Dancing like Babba with sparkly green eyes,
hunting for God in the color of skies.
Babba and I went hunting today.
We laughed and saw God; it was a good day.

Dear Grown–up,

You can use the story of Honey and Babba to help your children explore their feelings. For many children, explaining the feelings of Honey or Babba will be easier than expressing their own. Helping the children in our lives develop a vocabulary of "feeling words" is a wonderful gift. This page was designed by the Florida Hospital Cancer Institute to help you do just that. As you engage your children in discussion, you may even discover a fresh new way of viewing life—from a child's perspective. God bless you.

——*Stacy Barton and the Florida Hospital Cancer Institute*

- Why do you think Babba doesn't have any hair?

- Do you know what cancer is?

- Do you know someone who has cancer? Tell me about that.

- Why do you think Honey thought this day was a good day?

- If you were Honey, which part of this day would be your favorite? Tell me about it.

- What did Honey and Babba find when they went "hunting"?

- How do you think seeing the really big sunset made them feel? How did it make you feel?

- Do you think it helped Honey and Babba to know that God understands sadness and knows about fear?

- Are you afraid that Babba might die? What do you think it means to die?

- Have you ever known anyone who died? Were you sad? Were the people you love sad?

- What do you think makes Babba sad? How about Honey?

- What makes you feel sad? What makes you feel afraid?

- If God knows about Honey's sadness and fear, do you think he knows about yours? How does that make you feel?

- How many different feelings can you find in this story? Describe the different feelings, and we can name them together.

- Babba goes "hunting for God in the color of skies." Draw a picture of where you see God.